This book belongs to:

_____

SCOUT MOORE

Junior Ranger

YELLOWSTONE

Written by **THERESA HOWELL**
Illustrated by **JEFFREY EBBELER**

muddy boots™

we jump in puddles

GUILFORD, CONNECTICUT

My name is Scout Moore. I am WILD about the great outdoors.

I like to fish and swim.

I like to hike and bike.

My little brother, Wesley, and I count all
the birds that fly into our backyard.
"There's a new one!" Wesley shouts.
"That's a raven," I inform him. "The most
intelligent bird in the animal kingdom."

"Load 'em up, kids!"

Dad calls out.

"We're going to Yellowstone
National Park!" Mom says.

"Yellowstone National Park!" I
exclaim. "The first national park
ever? The one where it all began?"

"Yes!" Mom and Dad cheer.

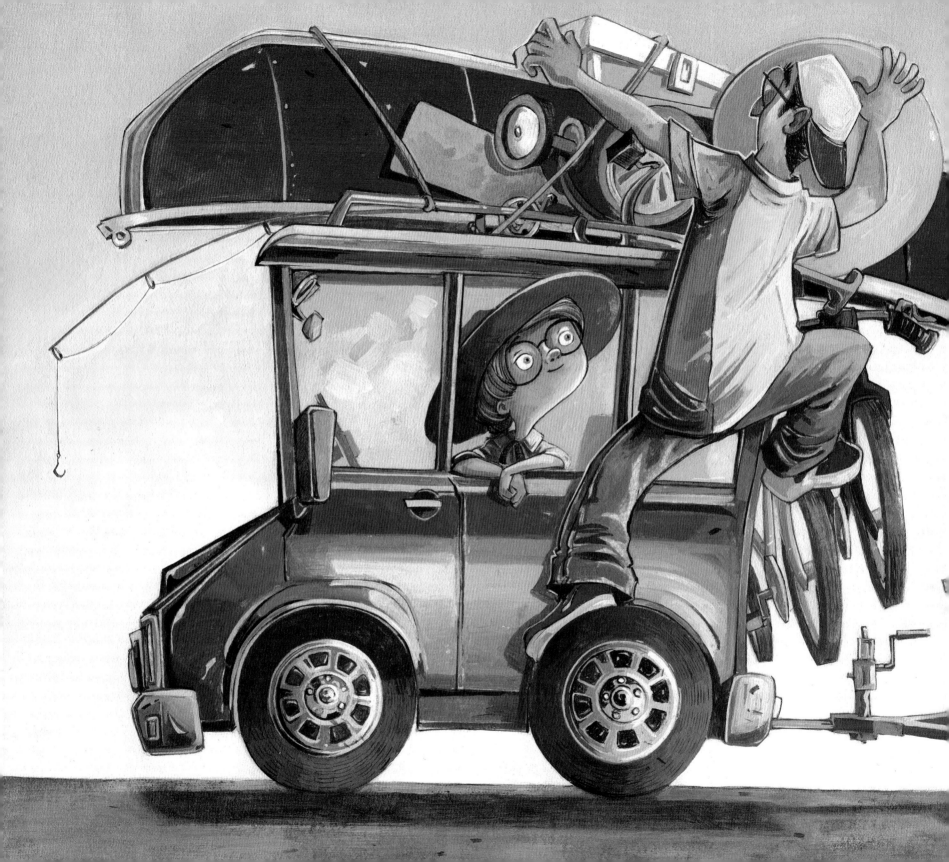

"Will we see bison?" I ask.
"Hopefully," answers Dad.
"Will we see any dragons?" Wesley asks.
"Hopefully NOT," Mom replies.

On our way to the park, we drive alongside rivers.
We pass under the shadows of mountains.
"Do you know what I want to see?" Mom says.
"What?"
"A moose," she says smiling. "I've always wanted
to see a moose."
"I've always wanted to see a dragon,"
Wesley says.

"There's the sign for Yellowstone National Park!" I shout.

"Picture time!" Dad says.

We stretch our legs and smile our biggest smiles.

"Everybody say 'Geothermal Features!'" Mom says.

First stop! The Junior Ranger Station!
We stand outside under a flag waving in
the breeze.

I'm so inspired I feel like I could soar
above this meadow, the mountains, and
the pines.

"This is the spot where the idea for
national parks was born," Ranger Bob
informs us.

"The greatest idea ever," I add.

The land around us hisses and steams.
It's white. It's rusty.
Up ahead there's a giant blue pool with red
and yellow tentacles.
Grand Prismatic Spring is almost too
beautiful to be real.
"What planet is this?" Wesley asks.
"Oh, this is our planet alright," Mom says.
"In all its glory."

"Old Faithful is going to erupt soon!" I yell.

Sputter.
Blow!
"WHOA!"

I time the eruption on my stopwatch and calculate when the next one is supposed to happen, just like a REAL ranger.

We wind along a wooden path through a land speckled with springs and pools.

"When is the best time to see a moose?" Mom asks.

"It says here that moose come out at dusk."

"Dragons, too," Wesley adds.

Just then, an eagle swoops down and pulls a fish from the lake with its talons.

"Now I've seen it all," Dad says.

BE BEAR AWARE

The ground bubbles, slurps, wheezes, and pops.

Up ahead lies a deep, dark, grumbly cave.

Suddenly, a puff of hot steam billows out of the cave's mouth.

"There *IS* a dragon here! I knew it!" Wesley shouts.

"A really smelly one!" Mom adds.

I know it's really hot steam from a spring inside the cave, but I'll let them believe it's a dragon—at least for a little while.

When we get to the valley, Dad pulls out our picnic basket and I pull out my binoculars.

There before our eyes, we see a herd of majestic bison. They are awesome and we know not to get too close.

"I see swans!" Wesley shouts.

"And elk!" Dad adds.

"Is that a moose?" Mom asks excitedly.
I turn my binoculars toward where
she's pointing.

"Sorry, Mom, it's just a fallen tree."

I hold my mom's hand as we stare
in awe at Lower Falls and the Grand
Canyon of the Yellowstone.
"I think this is the prettiest picture
nature has ever painted," I say.
And for a moment, all of us stand
silent, just soaking in the view.

Back at the Junior Ranger Station, Wesley
and I take the Junior Ranger Pledge and
receive our official patches.

"Thank you so much, Ranger Bob," I say.
"Can I ask you a question?"

"Of course," he says with a smile.

"Where's the best place to see a moose?"

He bends down
and whispers in my ear.
"Really!?" I say.

As a Yellowstone Junior Ranger, I promise to learn all I can to help preserve and protect Yellowstone's wildlife, history, and natural features. When I get home, I will teach others how to protect the natural world.

Yellowstone is home to many wild animals—bison, bears, birds, cougars, coyotes, frogs, fish, snakes, and more. In order to protect the wildlife at the park, it's important to keep a safe distance from all of the animals you see. They need their space and freedom. You also protect yourself because wild animals can be dangerous. Plus, you will have the amazing opportunity to view animals in their natural habitat.

In 1872 Yellowstone was established as America's first national park and since then thousands of people have traveled to the park to enjoy its natural beauty. But for 11,000 years before that, humans have been traveling through and living on these lands. The history of Yellowstone is long and important. By visiting and caring for the park, you, too, become a part of its history.

People travel from all over the world to see the unique natural features of Yellowstone National Park. Geysers, mudpots, hot springs, and fumeroles are called hydrothermal features. "Hydro" means water and "thermal" means hot. Stay on the boardwalks and don't get too close or you could be in hot water!

For Mom,
who always wanted to see a moose.
I love you so much.

         —T. H.

For Jack and Molly.

         —J. E.

Published by Muddy Boots
An imprint of The Rowman & Littlefield Publishing Group, Inc.
4501 Forbes Blvd., Ste. 200
Lanham, MD 20706
www.rowman.com

MuddyBootsBooks.com

Distributed by NATIONAL BOOK NETWORK

Copyright © 2019 Theresa Howell
Illustrations © 2019 Jeffrey Ebbeler

British Library Cataloguing in Publication Information available

Library of Congress Cataloging-in-Publication Data available

ISBN 978-1-63076-345-9 (hardcover)
ISBN 978-1-63076-354-1 (e-book)

Printed in China